**for Eleanor Appleton
and Oliver Schoonmaker
Thank you for passing along
your love of Books,
Birds,
and Odd Words.**

www.houghtonmifflinbooks.com

The text of this book is set in Mrs Eaves.
The illustrations were done in acrylic.

Library of Congress Cataloging-in-Publication Data

Brown, Calef.
 Soup for breakfast : a collection of pictures and poems / written and illustrated by Calef Brown.
 p. cm.
 ISBN 978-0-618-91641-2
 1. Children's poetry, American. I. Title.
 PS3552.R68525S68 2008
 811'.54—dc22
 2007047734

Printed in China
C&C 10 9 8 7 6 5 4 3 2 1

CONTENTS

BEAR PAWS

I wish I had bear paws
instead of hands.
No one understands.
Yes, there would be flaws,
but I could use my claws
to open cans,
and giant clams.
I could catch salmon
with my bare hands—
I mean my bare *paws*.
My bear paws.

T.P.L.T.T.F.

The Parking Lot That Time Forgot.
I kid you not, it does exist.
Clear your mind and picture this:
An endless sea of old sedans
with rumble seats and window fans,
classic coupes, and vintage vans—
in perfect rows they idle there,
completely free of wear and tear.
With lights aglow they seem to stare
from every space and every spot
in The Parking Lot That Time Forgot.

OILCLOTH TABLECLOTH

Oilcloth Tablecloth
keeps the table dry,
despite the many soda spills
and coffee gone awry.
If someone sloshes orange juice
or baby starts to cry,
Oilcloth Tablecloth
keeps the table dry.

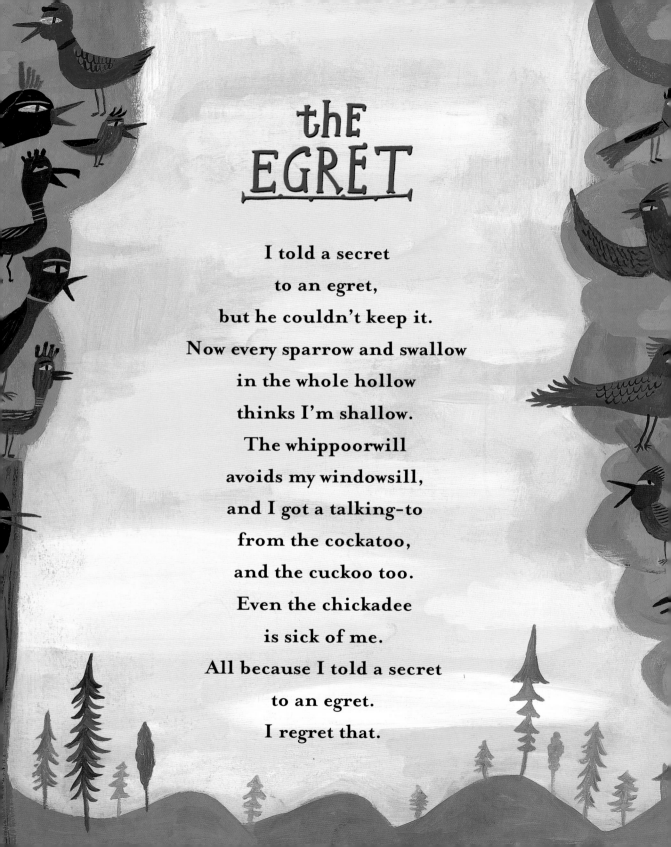

thE EGRET

I told a secret
to an egret,
but he couldn't keep it.
Now every sparrow and swallow
in the whole hollow
thinks I'm shallow.
The whippoorwill
avoids my windowsill,
and I got a talking-to
from the cockatoo,
and the cuckoo too.
Even the chickadee
is sick of me.
All because I told a secret
to an egret.
I regret that.

ARCHITOTS

Lots and lots of architects
begin their lives as "architots."
(Clever kids with wooden blocks
building houses, schools, and shops.)
See them raising rows of flats,
art museums, and laundromats.
What will they imagine next?
Future famous architects.

SOUP FOR BREAKFAST

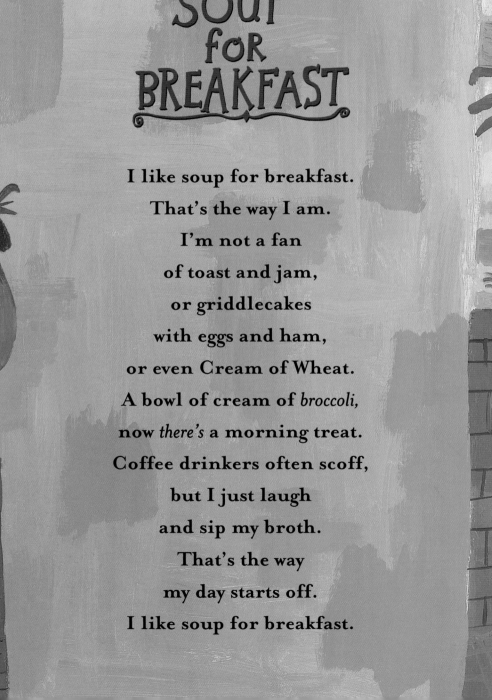

I like soup for breakfast.
That's the way I am.
I'm not a fan
of toast and jam,
or griddlecakes
with eggs and ham,
or even Cream of Wheat.
A bowl of cream of *broccoli*,
now *there's* a morning treat.
Coffee drinkers often scoff,
but I just laugh
and sip my broth.
That's the way
my day starts off.
I like soup for breakfast.

KITTYCAT

Kittycat does not like heat.
When the weather gets hot
she lies down flat.
When I say flat,
I mean just that—
two dimensional.
This is intentional,
because when the temperature drops
and back she pops
into the third dimension,
Kittycat gets treats
and lots of attention.

GRANDPA'S MUSTACHE

Grandpa has nose hair—
it really grows there.
It grows,
and grows,
and grows,
so much so
that people suppose
that Grandpa
must have a mustache,
since he waxes it,
so it cracks a bit
when he laughs.
It also makes him snore,
but Grandma doesn't care.
She can't hear.
Too much ear hair.

TONGUE TESTER

"Stealthy thieves
in knit wool caps
collect antiques
in thick cloth sacks."

Say this sentence
ten times fast.
People gasp
and often ask
if such a task
can harm the tongue,
or bust a lung,
or make a person
highly strung.
I really rather doubt it . . .
unless, of course,
you shout it.

PAINTING ON TOAST

Thank you for joining me.
I'll be your host.
The name of the program
is "Painting on Toast."
Before getting started,
we need to prepare.
The primer is butter.
Apply it with care.
Blueberry jam
makes a beautiful sky.
Brush on some cream cheese
for clouds going by.
Honey is dandy
for mountains and hills.
Mix it with cinnamon.
Show off your skills.

Now for a barn
with a silo and shed.
Raspberry jelly
is perfectly red.
Our painting is done,
except for the sun—
a dab of orange marmalade.
Look at the farm we made!

thE MARK

The mark of our intelligence
is how we treat the elephants,
the ocelots, the malamutes,
and other fellow residents.
We must protect the bandicoots,
orangutans, and pelicans.
The mark of our intelligence
is how we treat the elephants.

DONUTS

Why do all grownups
like donuts so much?
They rave about flavors
and fillings and such.
They praise all the glazes.
They savor the dough.
Donuts are tasty.
We get it!
We know!!

ONE to TEN
(and BACK AGAIN)

One, Two, close your eyes.
Think of something strange:
Fog that isn't foggy.
A day that doesn't change.

Three, Four, nod your head.
Think of something odd:
Underwater butterflies.
Fuzzy-wuzzy cod.

Five, Six, snap your fingers.
Think of something weird:
Noodles in a haystack.
A baby with a beard.

Seven, Eight, clap your hands.
Think of something silly:
Chickens popping bubble wrap.
Statues eating chili.

Nine, Ten, tap your feet.
Think of something fun:
Mulling over foolish whims.
Counting back to One.

YOUNG MOTH

Go forth,
Young Moth.
It takes strength
to lift up and stay aloft
with wings so soft.
Once in flight,
be swift,
or drift all night.
Return to earth
when lights go off.
Sleep tight,
Young Moth.